World of WarCraft

TRADING CARD GAME

The Art of the Trading Card Game

VOLUME ONE

The Art of the Trading Card Game

VOLUME ONE

Forewords by Samwise & Glenn Rane

CHRONICLE BOOKS

SAN FRANCISCO

ISBN: 978-0-8118-6193-9

Design by The Upper Deck Entertainment Creative Group
and Rise-and-Shine Studio, www.rise-and-shinestudio.com
Manufactured in China

First Edition 2008

Library of Congress Cataloging in Publication Data Available

Published by Chronicle Books LLC
680 Second Street
San Francisco, California 94107
www.chroniclebooks.com

Contents

mail from the Creative Development Associate Producer in charge of Product Development on the *AOTWOWTCG* (*Art of the World of Warcraft Trading Card Game*) project:

Dearest Mr. Didier,
Would you fancy writing an introduction for the Art of the World of Warcraft Trading Card Game*? It will need to be at least 750 words, but you can go all the way up to 2,000 words if you like.*

Would I "fancy"? What the heck am I possibly going to write about? Don't we have writers to do the writing here? No? I'm on my own? Well, then, here goes:

[Cue some epic Level 70 Elite Tauren Chieftain power metal]

Not long ago, artisans from all over the known realms were called forth to help create this work of sheer wonder. Talented painters and pixel-pushers who spent years and years in the industry earning their chops were called upon to lend their skills to this noble cause. Imagine all this talent and knowledge on one project—experienced professionals dealing with time-tested techniques and the tried-and-true core artistic foundations of proportion, perspective, lighting, and color theory. . . .

Then imagine a flying sidekick wearing black-and-blue plate mail screaming in and delivering a well-placed boot to the throat of that—hold on, hold on. I may be getting ahead of myself. I'm assuming that you are familiar with the artistic style of Blizzard Entertainment® and its products. If you *are*, then you're like Fonzie, baby: coooool. If you're not, here are a few suggestions you might consider:

(1) Keep reading this junk.
(2) Jump ahead to the fine works contained in this tome of epic artistic creation.
(3) All of the above.

Still here? All right, then, here we go. . . .

Here at Blizzard, our artists are hand-selected out of hundreds of candidates. Over the course of time they are beaten down with our universal artistic truths. Blizzard art (and especially that of *Warcraft*) has a distinct style and feeling about it. It takes an artist months to get all this down to the point where it becomes part of his or her artistic nature. Some of the basics that Blizzard artists learn:

(1) Less is NEVER more.
(2) Bigger is ALWAYS better.
(3) All one-handed weapons should be (at least) as big as two-handed weapons.
(4) If all else fails, add skulls and spikes and paint it red.

All our artists care about is the art. Is it cool? Does it kick ass over all others? We don't really worry about things like proportion or if it "would really work" in the real (boring) world. For example, just because a tauren wears shoulder pads that are so big that they don't allow him to go through revolving doors or drive compact cars doesn't mean that we need to shrink them down or make them functional. As long as the art looks amazing, we don't care if it doesn't look real or act like it would in the real world. Anyway, tauren ride kodo beasts and wouldn't care about sissy little econoboxes. In fact, cars like that are so small, we wouldn't even consider *them* for his shoulder pads. We would have to add skulls. We would even have to add spikes. I would hold off on painting them red, though—that might look too silly.

So, as you can see, learning how to draw like Blizzard is a task in itself—not something that comes easy. But these guys are straight-up professional pen-slingers who unleashed their magics upon us with great results. It wasn't uncommon to hear comments like "killer pose" or "badass lighting on those econobox shoulder pads" floating out of the art-review meetings.

Unfortunately, the celebration was the calm before the storm. The most gut-wrenching stage was yet to come. We like to call this perfect storm the Blizzard Art Approval Process. What this process consists of is the constant reworking of one piece of art till it's done. Then, once it's done, we go over it again just to make sure it truly is done. If there's more than one piece, the lucky artist gets a double shot—one of hell and the other of torment. But after months of working with these patient, artistic saints, we always hit a point where we're seeing the latest art submissions and saying, "Wow, that is . . . uhhh . . . really good. How'd he do that?" or "Holy crap, that's better than yours, man!" The art contained within this book is simply amazing in its energy and creativity. And the bulk of it was done by artists outside of Blizzard who had to emulate a style that isn't exactly easy to master. Well done, good people.

In closing, I need to offer many thanks (and hundreds of apologies) to all the kickass artists who helped bring this project to life with their artistic skills. I realize that you had to endure countless nitpicks about things being "too small" or "not red enough," and also an insane number of comments along the lines of, "It's just not feeling like *Warcraft*." The end result, though, has been amazing, and the latest rounds of art for future TCG releases have been looking even better. (I might even be so bold as to say that they've been feeling more "*Warcraft*" than ever!) Thanks again, cohorts of the pen, brush, and pixel.

For the Horde!!!

Samwise Didier
Senior Art Director, Blizzard Entertainment®

ith the success of *World of Warcraft*, more and more people and companies (at least in the gaming industry) seem to be paying attention to Blizzard's general business philosophy. In fact, more than a few times I've heard the phrase, "What would Blizzard do?" Here's a little story that Nick Carpenter, the company's cinematic creative director, was telling me about one of his first days here at Blizzard back in 1994 that might help us find the answer to that question.

> One day, Nick was painting a rock. He asked Samwise Didier (Sammy) what he thought of the rock. Sammy simply said, "Is that the best rock you can paint?" Nick knew that it was not, and he went back to work, painting the best rock he could paint.

the End

We have a term we throw around here called "Blizzard Quality." What this quality means to me is meeting and exceeding people's expectations. It's putting our full effort into making whatever it is we're making the best it can possibly be—even a rock. This level of quality is what everyone at Blizzard and Upper Deck has striven for with the making of this trading card game. We have an obligation to our players and to ourselves to give our best. If people can do something the right way and to the best of their abilities when they have the opportunity to do so, but they fail to try their hardest, what's the point of doing it at all? When it comes down to it, Blizzard employees are Blizzard gamers: We want to make cool games that we ourselves would like to play. It helps that we have a lot of people here who are really good at defining exactly what they want . . . [ahem] at least most of the time.

As you'll see, the art is phenomenal. We have the most talented artists in the world working on the *World of Warcraft Trading Card Game* (TCG). Being an artist myself, I am humbled and amazed daily by the skill the artists have exhibited from sketch to final, not to mention their professionalism and patience with our process. As Sammy D pointed out, we demand a lot.

When we set out on this project, the goal—as with everything we produce—was to showcase that familiar Blizzard Quality. Every piece of art had to look like it came from the *Warcraft* universe—a universe of over-proportioned characters, thick armor, huge weapons, and even larger shoulder pads. The artists at Blizzard have spent years developing and refining the *Warcraft* style. Consequently, it was important to us that each piece (besides looking damned cool!) stand up on its own as being inherently *Warcraft*, without borders and logos, and not be confused with any other fantasy license.

For example, the orcs from other fantasy universes aren't the same as the orcs of *Warcraft*, in either appearance or mentality. Therein lies the challenge! It's not always easy for artists who have worked in other fantasy universes to adapt to the *Warcraft* style. What looks like a generic minotaur at first glance is actually a different blend of man and bull entirely. There were, and are, many corrections: "Tauren have two fingers and a thumb. Gnomes are around 3.5 gnome heads tall. We need bigger *Warcraft*-looking shoulder pads . . . no, bigger! Oh, and more red!" Little swords and short-eared elves have reigned supreme for the past couple of decades in the fantasy genre, which makes *Warcraft* kind of odd and possibly silly-looking to new eyes. Spend some time in Azeroth, however, and you will get used to it!

In addition to the artists who painted cards for us, I'd like to mention and thank some other unsung heroes who made all the art in this book possible in the first place: specifically, the artists on the *World of Warcraft* development team. And by the way, not all artists use brushes and paint pictures, mind you. These artists are the designers of all the armor, weapons, creatures, buildings, dungeons, and environments. They are the animators who give life to the characters and monsters. They are the programmers who give the game its foundation. They are the writers who create the stories. And they are the game designers who make playing the game so much fun.

All of these elements have coalesced to make the best massively multiplayer online game to date, which has inspired other *World of Warcraft* products such as the *World of Warcraft TCG*. So, to all my brothers and sisters who have worked on *World of Warcraft*, past and present, thanks for your inspiration. We owe it all to you.

Dude! You forgot to turn off your stereo!

[End epic L70ETC power metal]

Glenn Rane
Creative Development Art Lead, Blizzard Entertainment®
Blizzard Art Director for the *World of Warcraft TCG*

nce in a great while—among all the clutter—something astonishing happens. Whether it's a great book, movie, or game, it seems to be a combination of the right things at the right time. You know it when you see it. *World of Warcraft®* is a perfect example of what I'm talking about. The arrival of the Internet—along with great art and gameplay—is what made it possible. I remember playing *World of Warcraft* for the first time and being blown away by the amazing game Blizzard Entertainment® had created. Beyond the superb game mechanics, *World of Warcraft*'s depth and fantastic setting made it a world where people wanted to lose themselves.

When I started working on the *World of Warcraft Trading Card Game* (*TCG*), I wanted fans to feel that same sense of awe—that we were delivering an unprecedented level of effort and passion in this project. Besides a great play experience, the art had to be something special. This couldn't be any old generic fantasy art; it had to be epic. As I explained to one illustrator, "Think of this as fantasy art on steroids." They say a picture is worth a thousand words, but I think each *World of Warcraft TCG* illustration is worth at least two thousand.

Our vision for the *TCG* was to make each card a window into the *Warcraft* universe. Being able to see your favorite *World of Warcraft* characters painted on a card is like having the ability to zoom in and see all the details of that character in high-definition. It's similar to what Alex Ross does for superheroes: You no longer have to imagine what a character or creature might look like because the artists captured what exists amorphously in every player's imagination.

Knowing that the art would bring this game to life, a lot of thought went into selecting which artists would work on this project. We wanted to work with artists whose work and attention to detail were just as amazing as the game whose universe they'd soon be joining. Alex Horley Orlandelli's cover paintings for *Heavy Metal* magazine, along with his work on *Mutant Chronicles* and *Lobo*, convinced us that he was one of the artists we wanted on the team. He has a great blend of comic-book exaggeration and solid classical-painting skills that make his illustrations come alive. Look for his work inside this book, and see if you agree. We also wanted people like Kev Walker and Jim Murray, both of whom were comic-book artists and fantasy painters. Jim Murray's painted *Batman/Judge Dredd* graphic novel is a great example of this balance between painting and comic-book art.

Todd McFarlane was also high on the list. The attitude, design, and attention to detail he brought to *Spawn* and all of his projects were the same sort of qualities we wanted him to bring to this TCG. In Todd's hands, a night elf hunter with 28 health is no longer just a night elf hunter with 28 health. Look at his illustration of Elendril (page 67)—with the long white hair and slender build—and you'll see how he brought this character to life. In terms of attitude, you see that not only can this guy shoot a bow, but he also gets to ride a tiger. This is what I'm talking about, and it doesn't end with just the figure: There are also really interesting shadow shapes in the background and great brush strokes in the foreground. Unless you're missing a pulse, you can't help but take a real interest in this night elf after seeing the art; I imagine that you'd even want to put him in a deck. This happens again and again, with every single card image and with every single artist. They have their own individual talents, and their artistic interpretations are what really make this game extraordinary.

This wasn't just any TCG we were creating, however, so we knew we needed more than just great art for the *World of Warcraft TCG*. Our goal was to create a seamless experience for both the *World of Warcraft* online player and the TCG player. This meant that every detail of each illustration would have to be meticulously examined and debated. Here are a few examples of what I'm talking about:

"This gnome doesn't look like a *World of Warcraft* gnome. Let's get a new sketch that's more accurate." [1 ; see facing page]

"Those breasts look way too large. Let's have the artist adjust the anatomy so it's more natural." [2]

"The axe should look more *World of Warcraft*—and let's see if the artist can adjust the size of the troll's head." [3]

Each piece of art was critiqued in this way before going to print. We want to bring you the best art possible, which is why we put so much effort into this game. I've traveled the globe attending comic conventions, reviewing portfolios, and meeting artists to make sure that only the best are creating images for this TCG. From Argentina, Britain, Croatia, France, and Germany to Hungary, Japan, Singapore, and the United States—some of the best artists from around the world created the art you're about to see.

Don't rush through this book by turning the pages too quickly. Take the time to really look at each image and absorb the details. I hope you enjoy all the hard work, dedication, and talent that went into making this book possible.

JEREMY CRANFORD
Creative Manager, Art Acquisition, *World of Warcraft TCG*
Upper Deck Entertainment

[1] Before | After

[2] Before | After

[3] Before | After

the Alliance

Throughout the history of Azeroth, the realities of war have driven imperiled cultures to form daring coalitions. Time and again, societies that might not otherwise see eye to eye have chosen to stand united and defiant in the face of overwhelming odds. Now, five bold races have formed a noble Alliance to hold firm against the inevitable return of the Burning Legion: The intrepid humans, enigmatic night elves, hardy dwarves, clever gnomes, and honorable draenei have all set aside their petty squabbles and pledged their lives in the fight to ensure the future safety of their world.

CARD NAME
Graccus
Azeroth 4 / 361

ARTIST
Doug Alexander

MEDIUM USED
Digital

CARD NAME
Girdle of Ulber
Azeroth 289 / 361

ARTIST
Phroilan Gardner

MEDIUM USED
Digital

CARD NAME

Killing Spree
Dark Portal 122 / 319

ARTIST
Greg Staples

MEDIUM USED
Digital

CARD NAME
Scorch
Dark Portal 53 / 319

ARTIST
Clint Langley

MEDIUM USED
Digital

CARD NAME
Shadowmistress Jezebel Hawke
Outland 143 / 246

ARTIST
Jonboy Meyers

MEDIUM USED
Digital

CARD NAME

Acolyte Demia
Azeroth 173 / 361

ARTIST
Mark Gibbons

MEDIUM USED
Digital

CARD NAME

Diplomacy
Dark Portal 128 / 319

ARTISTS
Zoltan Boros & Gabor Szikszai

MEDIUM USED
Mixed (Acrylic + Digital)

20

CARD NAME

Divine Shield
Azeroth 67 / 361

ARTIST
Matt Dixon

MEDIUM USED
Digital

CARD NAME

Slice and Dice
Dark Portal 89 / 319

ARTIST
Aleksi Briclot

MEDIUM USED
Digital

CARD NAME

Spiritual Healing
Azeroth 90 / 361

ARTIST
Dan Scott

MEDIUM USED
Digital

CARD NAME
Wynelh Harridan
Azeroth 224 / 361

ARTIST
Gabe from *Penny Arcade*

MEDIUM USED
Digital

CARD NAME
Lt. Commander Dudefella
Azeroth 203 / 361

ARTIST
Gabe from *Penny Arcade*

MEDIUM USED
Digital

CARD NAME

Leeroy Jenkins

Azeroth 198 / 361

ARTIST

Gabe from *Penny Arcade*

MEDIUM USED

Digital

CARD NAME

Victoria Iaton
Dark Portal 8 / 319

ARTIST
Mauro Cascioli

MEDIUM USED
Digital

CARD NAME

Raul "Fingers" Maldren
Dark Portal 187 / 319

ARTIST
Cyril Van Der Haegen

MEDIUM USED
Digital

CARD NAME

Reverend Tobias
Dark Portal 188 / 319

ARTIST
William O'Connor

MEDIUM USED
Digital

CARD NAME
Undaunted Defense
Dark Portal 66 / 319

ARTIST
Kev Walker

MEDIUM USED
Gouache

CARD NAME

The Perfect Stout
Dark Portal 293 / 319

ARTIST
Marcelo Vignali

MEDIUM USED
Digital

CARD NAME
Retribution Aura
Azeroth 71 / 361

ARTIST
Glenn Rane

MEDIUM USED
Digital

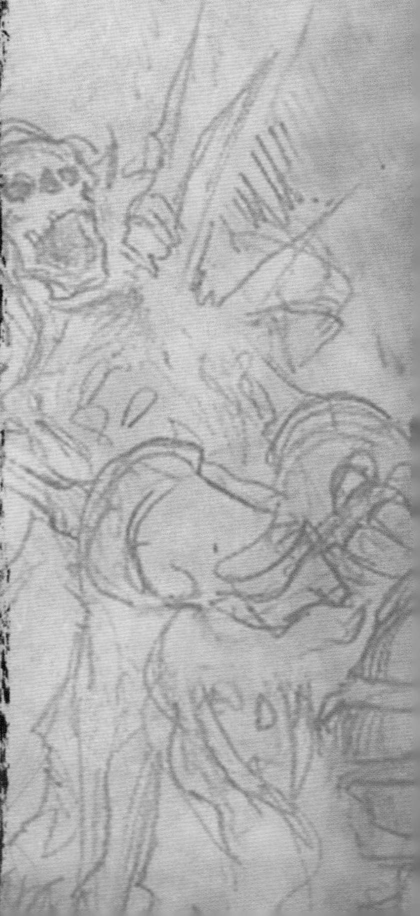

CARD NAME

Sal Grimstalker
Outland 141 / 246

ARTIST
Brian Despain

MEDIUM USED
Digital

CARD NAME
Nesmend Darkbreaker
Outland 134 / 246

ARTIST
Daren Bader

MEDIUM USED
Digital

CARD NAME
**When Smokey Sings,
I Get Violent**
Outland 246 / 246

ARTIST
Greg Staples

MEDIUM USED
Digital

GARD NAME

Ubel Sternbrow
Outland 148 / 246

ARTIST
Alex Horley Orlandelli

MEDIUM USED
Acrylic

CARD NAME

Pithran Mithrilshot
Dark Portal 185 / 319

ARTIST
Christopher Moeller

MEDIUM USED
Acrylic

CARD NAME
Savin Lightguard
Dark Portal 6 / 319

ARTISTS
Zoltan Boros & Gabor Szikszai

MEDIUM USED
Mixed (Acrylic + Digital)

CARD NAME
Lava Spit
Molten Core Raid 25 / 53

ARTIST
Ashley Wood

MEDIUM USED
Digital

CARD NAME
Kor Cindervein
Azeroth 192 / 361

ARTIST
Daren Bader

MEDIUM USED
Digital

CARD NAME
Durdin Hammerhand
Dark Portal 162 / 319

ARTIST
Dany Orizio

MEDIUM USED
Digital

CARD NAME
Gustaf Trueshot
Dark Portal 166 / 319

ARTIST
Christopher Moeller

MEDIUM USED
Acrylic

39

CARD NAME

Aspect of the Viper
Dark Portal 31 / 319

ARTIST
Artgerm

MEDIUM USED
Digital

CARD NAME

Dwarven Hand Cannon
Azeroth 319 / 361

ARTIST
Tyler Walpole

MEDIUM USED
Digital

CARD NAME

Last Stand
Azeroth 143 / 361

ARTIST

Michael Komarck

MEDIUM USED

Digital

CARD NAME

Grumpherys
Dark Portal 2 / 319

ARTIST
Kev Walker

MEDIUM USED
Gouache

44

CARD NAME

Prayer of Healing
Azeroth 84 / 361

ARTIST

Miguel Coimbra

MEDIUM USED

Digital

CARD NAME

Sunder Armor
Azeroth 149 / 361

ARTIST

Samwise

MEDIUM USED

Digital

CARD NAME
"Chipper" Ironbane
Dark Portal 160 / 319

ARTIST
E.M. Gist

MEDIUM USED
Oil

CARD NAME
Warrax
Azeroth 8 / 361

ARTIST
Dave Dorman

MEDIUM USED
Acrylic

CARD NAME
King Magni Bronzebeard
Azeroth 191 / 361

ARTIST
Andrew Robinson

MEDIUM USED
Acrylic

CARD NAME

Claw
Dark Portal 20 / 319

ARTIST
Dany Orizio

MEDIUM USED
Digital

CARD NAME
Slow
Outland 45 / 246

ARTIST
Wayne Reynolds

MEDIUM USED
Acrylic

49

CARD NAME
Mind Soothe
Outland 58 / 246

ARTIST
Dan Dos Santos

MEDIUM USED
Digital

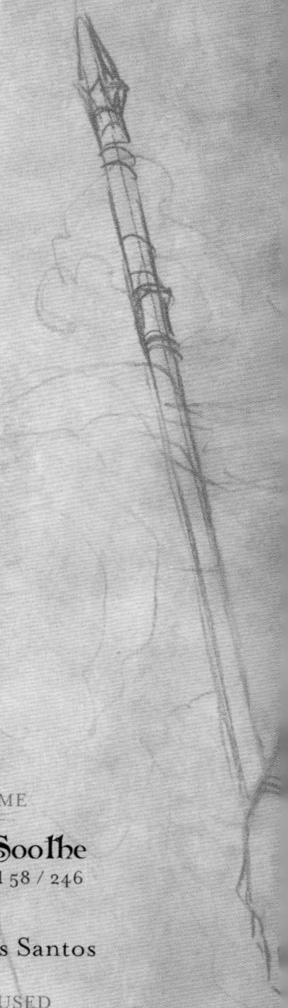

CARD NAME
Yanna Dai'shalan
Outland 9 / 246

ARTIST
Greg Staples

MEDIUM USED
Digital

CARD NAME

Innervate
Azeroth 23 / 361

ARTIST
Doug Alexander

MEDIUM USED
Digital

CARD NAME

Telrander
Dark Portal 7 / 319

ARTIST
Alex Horley Orlandelli

MEDIUM USED
Acrylic

CARD NAME
Avanthera
Dark Portal 154 / 319

ARTIST
Christopher Moeller

MEDIUM USED
Acrylic

CARD NAME
Kavai the Wanderer
Dark Portal 173 / 319

ARTIST
Jim Murray

MEDIUM USED
Acrylic

CARD NAME
Vigilance
Dark Portal 126 / 319

ARTIST
Wayne Reynolds

MEDIUM USED
Acrylic

CARD NAME
Latro Abiectus
Azeroth 197 / 361

ARTIST
Clint Langley

MEDIUM USED
Digital

CARD NAME
Fang of the Crystal Spider
Azeroth 320 / 361

ARTIST
Patrick McEvoy

MEDIUM USED
Digital

56

CARD NAME

Seva Shadowdancer
Azeroth 216 / 361

ARTIST
Clint Langley

MEDIUM USED
Digital

CARD NAME

Parren Shadowshot
Outland 136 / 246

ARTIST
Christopher Moeller

MEDIUM USED
Acrylic

CARD NAME

Renew
Dark Portal 77 / 319

ARTIST
Miguel Coimbra

MEDIUM USED
Digital

CARD NAME
Goldenmoon
Dark Portal 165 / 319

ARTIST
Wayne Reynolds

MEDIUM USED
Acrylic

CARD NAME
Tristan Rapidstrike
Azeroth 221 / 361

ARTIST
Alex Horley Orlandelli

MEDIUM USED
Acrylic

CARD NAME
Dual Wield
Dark Portal 127 / 319

ARTIST
Kev Walker

MEDIUM USED
Gouache

CARD NAME
Kailis Truearc
Azeroth 189 / 361

ARTIST
Doug Alexander

MEDIUM USED
Digital

CARD NAME

Neeka ›
Outland 133 / 246

ARTIST
James Zhang

MEDIUM USED
Digital

CARD NAME

Fury
Azeroth 38 / 361

ARTIST
Todd McFarlane

MEDIUM USED
Digital

CARD NAME

Flight Form
Outland 21 / 246

ARTIST
Brandon Kitkouski

MEDIUM USED
Digital

CARD NAME

Nathressa Darkstrider
Dark Portal 3 / 319

ARTIST
Dan Scott

MEDIUM USED
Digital

CARD NAME

Nalkas
Outland 131 / 246

ARTIST
Michael Komarck

MEDIUM USED
Digital

CARD NAME

Elendril
Azeroth 3 / 361

ARTIST
Todd McFarlane

MEDIUM USED
Digital

CARD NAME

Deadly Brew
Outland 65 / 246

ARTIST
Brian Despain

MEDIUM USED
Digital

CARD NAME

The Relics of Wakening
Dark Portal 296 / 319

ARTIST
Marcelo Vignali

MEDIUM USED
Digital

CARD NAME

Lobotomize
Azeroth 100 / 361

ARTIST
Glenn Rane

MEDIUM USED
Digital

CARD NAME
Mazar
Outland 4 / 246

ARTIST
Dan Scott

MEDIUM USED
Digital

CARD NAME
Sneak
Azeroth 152 / 361

ARTIST
Glenn Rane

MEDIUM USED
Digital

CARD NAME

Fillet, Kneecapper
Extraordinaire
Outland 2 / 246

ARTIST
Warren Mahy

MEDIUM USED
Digital

CARD NAME

Dizdemona
Azeroth 2 / 361

ARTIST
Gabe from *Penny Arcade*

MEDIUM USED
Digital

CARD NAME

Parvink
Azeroth 212 / 361

ARTIST
Samwise

MEDIUM USED
Digital

CARD NAME

Expose Armor
Azeroth 98 / 361

ARTIST
Mark Zug

MEDIUM USED
Oil

CARD NAME

Malfunction
Dark Portal 147 / 319

ARTIST
Ron Spears

MEDIUM USED
Digital

HORLEY

CARD NAME

Spellsteal
Dark Portal 54 / 319

ARTIST NAME
Alex Horley Orlandelli

MEDIUM USED
Acrylic

CARD NAME

Immolate
Outland 85 / 246

ARTIST
Alex Horley Orlandelli

MEDIUM USED
Acrylic

CARD NAME
Meekway Humzinger
Dark Portal 182 / 319

ARTIST
Daren Bader

MEDIUM USED
Digital

CARD NAME
Arcane Power
Dark Portal 44 / 319

ARTIST
Alex Horley Orlandelli

MEDIUM USED
Acrylic

Arcane Blast

ARTIST
Chippy

MEDIUM USED
Digital

CARD NAME

Timmo Shadestep

Azeroth 7 / 361

ARTIST
Glenn Rane

MEDIUM USED
Digital

Tinkmaster Overspark

Outland 144 / 246

Tom Baxa

Gouache

Finkle Einhorn, At Your Service!

Dark Portal 316 / 319

Jeff Miracola

Oil

CARD NAME
Chromatic Cloak
Azeroth 282 / 361

ARTIST
Tom Fleming

MEDIUM USED
Mixed (Watercolor + Color Pencil)

CARD NAME

Phadalus the Enlightened
Dark Portal 4 / 319

ARTIST
Glenn Rane

MEDIUM USED
Digital

CARD NAME
Vindicator Enkallus
Dark Portal 195 / 319

ARTIST
Sean O'Daniels

MEDIUM USED
Digital

CARD NAME

Kallipssa
Dark Portal 172 / 319

ARTISTS
Zoltan Boros & Gabor Szikszai

MEDIUM USED
Mixed (Acrylic + Digital)

CARD NAME

Totem of Coo
Outland 228 / 246

ARTIST
James Zhang

MEDIUM USED
Digital

CARD NAME

Moala Stonebinder
Outland 5 / 246

ARTIST
Christopher Moeller

MEDIUM USED
Acrylic

CARD NAME

Ozzali
Outland 6 / 246

ARTIST

James Zhang

MEDIUM USED

Digital

CARD NAME

Kana Nassis
Outland 3 / 246

ARTIST

Dermot Power

MEDIUM USED

Digital

The Horde

Once a name spoken only in fearful whispers, the mighty Horde has taken aggressive steps to shed its former reputation for wanton bloodshed and reckless expansionism. Under new leadership, these outcasts of Azeroth are now determined to secure their rightful place within it. The powerful orcs, shadowy undead, spiritual tauren, crafty trolls, and driven blood elves have all united under the banner of this newly inspired Horde. With unshakable resolve and renewed commitment, they heed the lessons of the past even as they forge ahead into an uncertain future.

Demoralizing Shout

Azeroth 140 / 361

ARTIST
Tristan Elwell

MEDIUM USED
Digital

CARD NAME

Spinal Reaper

Molten Core 28 / 30

ARTISTS
Zoltan Boros & Gabor Szikszai

MEDIUM USED
Mixed (Acrylic + Digital)

PHR01

CARD NAME

Frost Shock
Azeroth 109 / 361

ARTIST
Phroilan Gardner

MEDIUM USED
Digital

CARD NAME

Najan Spiritbinder
Outland 178 / 246

ARTIST

Volkan Baga

MEDIUM USED

Oil

CARD NAME

Kaal Soulreaper
Azeroth 245 / 361

ARTIST
Mark Gibbons

MEDIUM USED
Digital

CARD NAME

Eye of Rend
Azeroth 288 / 361

ARTIST
Mark Gibbons

MEDIUM USED
Digital

Dan Scott

CARD NAME

Snarl Hellwind
Outland 185 / 246

ARTIST
Dan Scott

MEDIUM USED
Digital

CARD NAME

Aegis of the Blood God
Dark Portal 247 / 319

ARTIST
Daren Bader

MEDIUM USED
Digital

CARD NAME

Zomm Hopeslayer
Outland 18 / 246

ARTIST
Kev Walker

MEDIUM USED
Gouache

CARD NAME

Kralnor
Dark Portal 220 / 319

ARTIST
Mauro Cascioli

MEDIUM USED
Digital

CARD NAME
Earth Shock
Dark Portal 82 / 319

ARTIST
Kevin Chin

MEDIUM USED
Digital

CARD NAME
Bloodlust
Outland 73 / 246

ARTISTS
Zoltan Boros & Gabor Szikszai

MEDIUM USED
Mixed (Acrylic + Digital)

CARD NAME
Flametongue Weapon
Dark Portal 95 / 319

ARTIST
Dan Dos Santos

MEDIUM USED
Oil

CARD NAME
Hotter Than Goo
Molten Core Raid 22 / 53

ARTIST
Jon Foster

MEDIUM USED
Digital

CARD NAME
Landro Longshot
Azeroth 278 / 361

ARTIST
Dan Scott

MEDIUM USED
Digital

CARD NAME

Windfury Totem

Azeroth 118 / 361

ARTIST

Dave Allsop

MEDIUM USED

Digital

CARD NAME

Hidden Enemies
Dark Portal 302 / 319

ARTIST
William O'Connor

MEDIUM USED
Digital

CARD NAME

Rexxar
Dark Portal 231 / 319

ARTIST
Samwise

MEDIUM USED
Digital

CARD NAME

Hur Shieldsmasher
Azeroth 243 / 361

ARTIST

Lucas Graciano

MEDIUM USED

Oil

CARD NAME
High Overlord Saurfang
Dark Portal 214 / 319

ARTIST
Dan Dos Santos

MEDIUM USED
Oil

CARD NAME
Warmaster Hork
Dark Portal 241 / 319

ARTIST
Dave Kendall

MEDIUM USED
Oil

CARD NAME
Commanding Shout
Dark Portal 118 / 319

ARTIST
Wayne Reynolds

MEDIUM USED
Acrylic

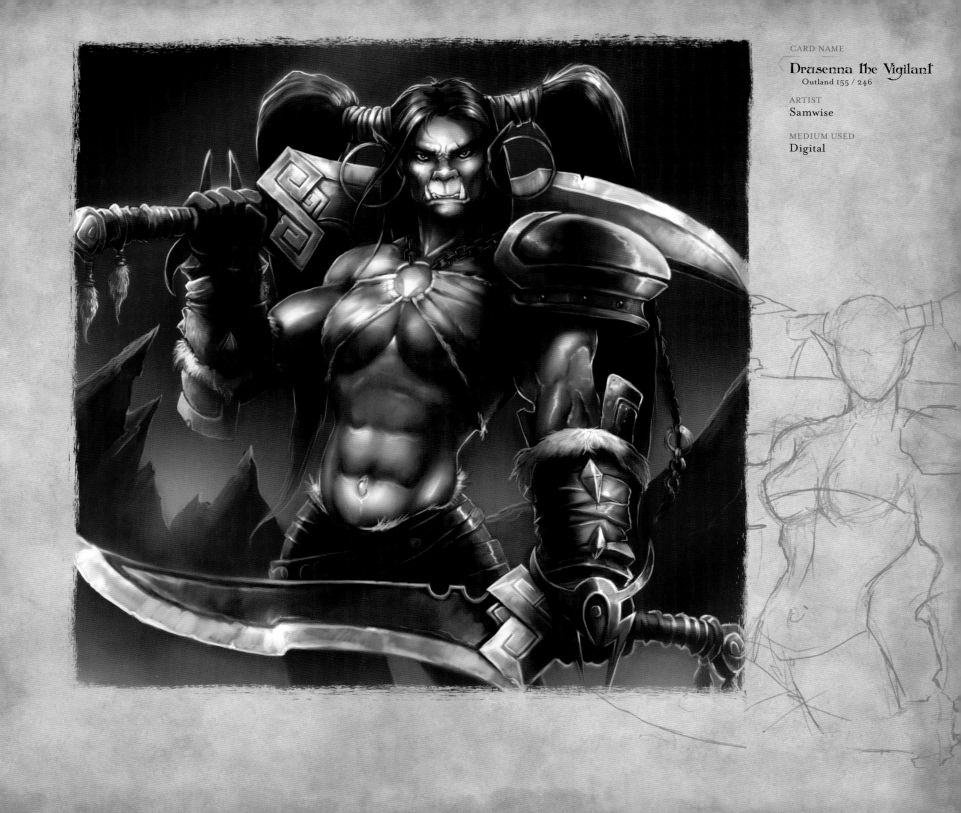

CARD NAME
Drasenna the Vigilant
Outland 155 / 246

ARTIST
Samwise

MEDIUM USED
Digital

CARD NAME
Zygore Bladebreaker
Azeroth 275 / 361

ARTIST
Michael Komarck

MEDIUM USED
Digital

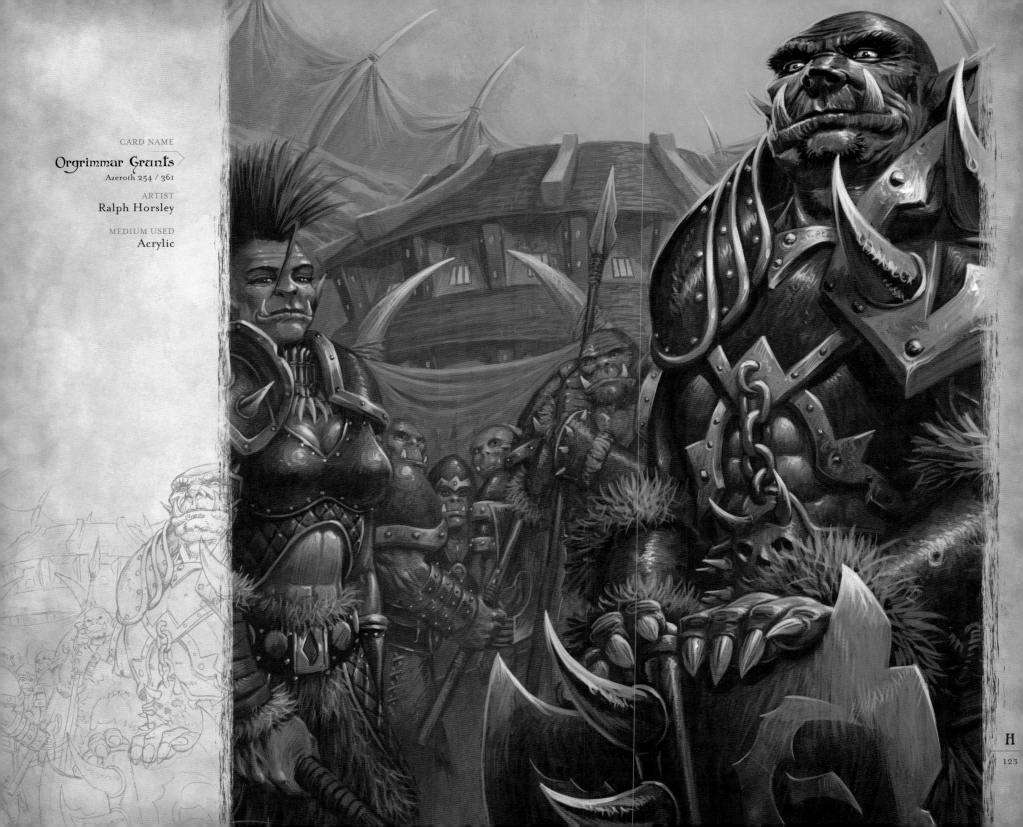

CARD NAME

Orgrimmar Grunts
Azeroth 254 / 361

ARTIST
Ralph Horsley

MEDIUM USED
Acrylic

H

CARD NAME
Outrider Zarg
Dark Portal 227 / 319

ARTIST
Paolo Parente

MEDIUM USED
Acrylic

CARD NAME
Challenging Shout
Dark Portal 117 / 319

ARTIST
Michael Sutfin

MEDIUM USED
Oil

CARD NAME

Stellaris
Outland 221 / 246

ARTIST
Clint Langley

MEDIUM USED
Digital

CARD NAME
Radak Doombringer
Azeroth 13 / 361

ARTIST
Greg Staples

MEDIUM USED
Oil

CARD NAME
Jackknife
Outland 69 / 246

ARTISTS
Zoltan Boros & Gabor Szikszai

MEDIUM USED
Mixed (Acrylic + Digital)

CARD NAME
Nyn'jah
Dark Portal 226 / 319

ARTIST
James Zhang

MEDIUM USED
Digital

CARD NAME

Predatory Gloves
Outland 203 / 246

ARTIST
Dany Orizio

MEDIUM USED
Digital

CARD NAME
Mojo Mender Ja'nah
Dark Portal 15 / 319

ARTIST
Jonboy Meyers

MEDIUM USED
Digital

CARD NAME
Blood Guard Mal'wani
Azeroth 230 / 361

ARTIST
Tom Baxa

MEDIUM USED
Oil

CARD NAME

Bad Mojo Mask

Azeroth 281 / 361

ARTIST

Clint Langley

MEDIUM USED

Digital

CARD NAME
Eskhandar's Right Claw
Molten Core 21 / 30

ARTIST
James Zhang

MEDIUM USED
Digital

CARD NAME

Zalazane
Dark Portal 310 / 319

ARTIST
Sean O'Daniels

MEDIUM USED
Digital

CARD NAME

Zy'lah Manslayer

Azeroth 276 / 361

ARTIST

Jonboy Meyers

MEDIUM USED

Digital

CARD NAME

Bloodrage
Dark Portal 116 / 319

ARTIST

Ron Spencer

MEDIUM USED

Mixed (Acrylic
+ Colored Pencil
+ Marker)

CARD NAME
Gz'lrin
Outland 158 / 246

ARTIST
Brian Despain

MEDIUM USED
Digital

CARD NAME

Indalamar
Outland 13 / 246

ARTIST
Michael Komarck

MEDIUM USED
Digital

CARD NAME
Sus'vayin
Outland 187 / 246

ARTIST
Kev Walker

MEDIUM USED
Gouache

CARD NAME

Ornate Adamantium
Breastplate
Dark Portal 259 / 319

ARTIST
Clint Langley

MEDIUM USED
Digital

CARD NAME

Greeter
Dark Portal 211 / 319

ARTIST
Mark Evans

MEDIUM USED
Digital

CARD NAME

**Gurubashi
Dwarf Destroyer**
Dark Portal 274 / 319

ARTIST
Samwise

MEDIUM USED
Digital

CARD NAME

Ra'chee

Dark Portal 230 / 319

ARTIST
Warren Mahy

MEDIUM USED
Digital

CARD NAME

Aspect of the Hawk

Azeroth 34 / 361

ARTIST
Phroilan Gardner

MEDIUM USED
Digital

CARD NAME

Taz'dingo

Azeroth 260 / 361

ARTIST
Alex Horley Orlandelli

MEDIUM USED
Acrylic

CARD NAME

Kulan Earthguard

Azeroth 249 / 361

ARTIST
Samwise

MEDIUM USED
Digital

CARD NAME
One-Thousand-Battles
Outland 181 / 246

ARTIST
Lucas Graciano

MEDIUM USED
Oil

CARD NAME
Stone Guard Rashun
Dark Portal 234 / 319

ARTIST
Carl Critchlow

MEDIUM USED
Acrylic

CARD NAME
Fire Elemental Totem
Outland 77 / 246

ARTIST
Lucas Graciano

MEDIUM USED
Oil

CARD NAME

Test of Faith
Dark Portal 308 / 319

ARTIST
James Zhang

MEDIUM USED
Digital

CARD NAME

Windseer Tarus
Azeroth 271 / 361

ARTISTS
Zoltan Boros & Gabor Szikszai

MEDIUM USED
Mixed (Acrylic + Digital)

CARD NAME

Grennan Stormspeaker
Azeroth 10 / 361

ARTIST
Samwise

MEDIUM USED
Digital

CARD NAME

Wrath
Dark Portal 30 / 319

ARTIST
Greg Staples

MEDIUM USED
Digital

CARD NAME

Morova of the Sands
Dark Portal 17 / 319

ARTIST
Todd Lockwood

MEDIUM USED
Digital

CARD NAME

Bulkas Wildhorn
Dark Portal 12 / 319

ARTIST NAME

Marcelo Vignali

MEDIUM USED
Digital

CARD NAME

Herod's Shoulder

Azeroth 293 / 361

ARTIST

Jonboy Meyers

MEDIUM USED

Digital

CARD NAME

Crushing Blow
Dark Portal 120 / 319

ARTIST
Dave Kendall

MEDIUM USED
Oil

CARD NAME

Tempest, Son—of—Storms
Outland 188 / 246

ARTIST
Alex Horley Orlandelli

MEDIUM USED
Acrylic

CARD NAME

Cleave
Azeroth 138 / 361

ARTIST
Phroilan Gardner

MEDIUM USED
Digital

CARD NAME

Rampage
Outland 96 / 246

ARTIST
Jim Murray

MEDIUM USED
Acrylic

CARD NAME
Tanwa the Marksman
Dark Portal 235 / 319

ARTIST
Daren Bader

MEDIUM USED
Digital

CARD NAME

Travel Form
Dark Portal 29 / 319

ARTIST
Lars Grant-West

MEDIUM USED
Digital

CARD NAME
Call of the Wild
Outland 19 / 246

ARTISTS
Zoltan Boros & Gabor Szikszai

MEDIUM USED
Mixed (Acrylic + Digital)

CARD NAME
Mind Vision
Dark Portal 75 / 319

ARTIST
Michael Komarck

MEDIUM USED
Digital

CARD NAME

The Haunted Mills
Dark Portal 301 / 319

ARTIST
Dave Allsop

MEDIUM USED
Digital

CARD NAME

Valthak Spiritdrinker
Azeroth 263 / 361

ARTIST
Jonboy Meyers

MEDIUM USED
Digital

CARD NAME

Mind Spike
Azeroth 82 / 361

ARTISTS
Zoltan Boros & Gabor Szikszai

MEDIUM USED
Mixed (Acrylic + Digital)

CARD NAME

Borlis Brode
Outland 153 / 246

ARTIST
Dave Allsop

MEDIUM USED
Digital

CARD NAME

Shawn of the Dead
Outland 183 / 246

ARTIST
Glenn Rane

MEDIUM USED
Digital

CARD NAME

Faith Healer's Boots
Outland 197 / 246

ARTIST
Dave Allsop

MEDIUM USED
Digital

CARD NAME
Omedus the Punisher
Azeroth 12 / 361

ARTIST
Jeff Miracola

MEDIUM USED
Oil

CARD NAME

Touch of Chaos
Dark Portal 284 / 319

ARTIST

Tom Baxa

MEDIUM USED

Oil

CARD NAME
Crown of Destruction
Dark Portal 252 / 319

ARTIST
Justin Sweet

MEDIUM USED
Digital

CARD NAME

Fizzle
Outland 40 / 246

ARTIST
James Zhang

MEDIUM USED
Digital

CARD NAME

Benethor Draigo
Azeroth 228 / 361

ARTIST
Alex Horley Orlandelli

MEDIUM USED
Acrylic

CARD NAME

Panax the Unstable
Azeroth 255 / 361

ARTIST

Clint Langley

MEDIUM USED

Digital

CARD NAME
Mordotz
Outland 175 / 246

ARTIST
Brian Despain

MEDIUM USED
Digital

CARD NAME
Erytheis
Outland 156 / 246

ARTIST
Artgerm

MEDIUM USED
Digital

H

177

CARD NAME

Deacon Johanna
Azeroth 234 / 361

ARTISTS
Zoltan Boros & Gabor Szikszai

MEDIUM USED
Mixed (Acrylic + Digital)

CARD NAME
Sister Rot
Dark Portal 233 / 319

ARTIST
Puddnhead

MEDIUM USED
Digital

CARD NAME
Berserker Rage
Outland 91 / 246

ARTISTS
Zoltan Boros & Gabor Szikszai

MEDIUM USED
Mixed (Acrylic + Digital)

CARD NAME

Dampen Magic
Dark Portal 48 / 319

ARTIST
Phroilan Gardner

MEDIUM USED
Digital

CARD NAME

A Donation of Silk
Dark Portal 314 / 319

ARTIST
Brandon Kitkouski

MEDIUM USED
Digital

CARD NAME

Fear
Azeroth 123 / 361

ARTIST
Mauro Cascioli

MEDIUM USED
Digital

CARD NAME
Shadowstrike
Molten Core 27 / 30

ARTIST
Wei Wang

MEDIUM USED
Digital

Jon Reaver
Outland 165 / 246

ARTIST
Sean O'Daniels

MEDIUM USED
Digital

CARD NAME

Charge
Azeroth 137 / 361

ARTIST
Alex Horley Orlandelli

MEDIUM USED
Acrylic

HORLEY

CARD NAME

Cannibalize
Dark Portal 136 / 319

ARTIST
Carl Critchlow

MEDIUM USED
Acrylic

CARD NAME

Pick Pocket
Outland 71 / 246

ARTIST
Alex Horley Orlandelli

MEDIUM USED
Acrylic

CARD NAME

Aleyah Dawnborn
Dark Portal 10 / 319

ARTIST
Todd Lockwood

MEDIUM USED
Digital

CARD NAME

Spiritual Attunement
Dark Portal 65 / 319

ARTIST
Yina

MEDIUM USED
Digital

CARD NAME

Jazmin Bloodlove
Outland 164 / 246

ARTISTS
Zoltan Boros & Gabor Szikszai

MEDIUM USED
Mixed (Acrylic + Digital)

CARD NAME

Blistering Fire
Dark Portal 46 / 319

ARTIST
Alex Horley Orlandelli

MEDIUM USED
Acrylic

Katsin Bloodoath

ARTIST
Theodore Park

MEDIUM USED
Digital

Tyrus Sheynathren
Dark Portal 238 / 319

ARTIST
Alex Horley Orlandelli

MEDIUM USED
Acrylic

CARD NAME
Seal of the Crusader
Dark Portal 64 / 319

ARTIST
Michael Komarck

MEDIUM USED
Digital

CARD NAME

Silencing Shot
Outland 35 / 246

ARTIST
Chippy

MEDIUM USED
Digital

CARD NAME

Sonic Spear
Outland 219 / 246

ARTIST
Ben Thompson

MEDIUM USED
Oil

CARD NAME
Araelan
Dark Portal 198 / 319

ARTIST
UDON

MEDIUM USED
Digital

CARD NAME
Molten Armor
Outland 44 / 246

ARTIST
Brandon Kitkouski

MEDIUM USED
Digital

CARD NAME

Tiril Dawnrider
Dark Portal 237 / 319

ARTIST
Greg Staples

MEDIUM USED
Digital

Monsters & Locations

Long ago, the colossal titans set about the art of creation and shaped the tranquil world of Azeroth. They charged mighty dragons with safeguarding the burgeoning world as plants, trees, and creatures of every kind began to evolve and thrive. Over time, cataclysms attributable to both man and magic left their scars upon the land. But myriad life-forms have stubbornly maintained their grasp, not only on Azeroth, but in the fragmented realm of Outland as well. Together these worlds provide a seemingly endless landscape filled with beauty, danger, and unparalleled opportunities for adventure.

CARD NAME
The Love Potion
Azeroth 356 / 361

ARTIST
Clint Langley

MEDIUM USED
Digital

Spirit Healer
Azeroth 169 / 361

Mark Gibbons

Digital

CARD NAME
Helwen
Azeroth 126 / 361

ARTIST
Dave Kendall

MEDIUM USED
Oil

CARD NAME
Big Game Hunter
Azeroth 348 / 361

ARTIST
James Zhang

MEDIUM USED
Digital

CARD NAME
Noggenfogger Elixir
Azeroth 309 / 361

ARTIST
Sean O'Daniels

MEDIUM USED
Digital

CARD NAME
The Hammer of Grace
Azeroth 323 / 361

ARTIST
Patrick McEvoy

MEDIUM USED
Digital

CARD NAME
Inventor's Focal Sword
Azeroth 330 / 361

ARTIST
Patrick McEvoy

MEDIUM USED
Digital

CARD NAME

Infernal
Azeroth 127 / 361

ARTISTS
Zoltan Boros & Gabor Szikszai

MEDIUM USED
Mixed (Acrylic + Digital)

CARD NAME

Forbidden Knowledge
Azeroth 124 / 361

ARTIST
Greg Staples

MEDIUM USED
Digital

CARD NAME

Battle Shout
Azeroth 135 / 361

ARTIST
Mauro Cascioli

MEDIUM USED
Digital

CARD NAME

> Destiny
>
> Azeroth 318 / 361

ARTIST
Ryan Sook

MEDIUM USED
Digital

CARD NAME

Teeba's Blazing Longsword
Azeroth 335 / 361

ARTIST
Jason Engle

MEDIUM USED
Digital

CARD NAME

Foolish Mortals!
Onyxia Raid 16 / 33

ARTIST
Steve Ellis

MEDIUM USED
Oil

CARD NAME

Tail Swipe
Onyxia Raid 26 / 33

ARTIST
Mauro Cascioli

MEDIUM USED
Digital

CARD NAME

Bellowing Roar
Onyxia Raid 5 / 33

ARTIST
Miguel Coimbra

MEDIUM USED
Digital

M&L

218

CARD NAME
Dragon Hide
Onyxia Raid 13 / 33

ARTIST
Miguel Coimbra

MEDIUM USED
Digital

CARD NAME
Crash
Onyxia Raid 8 / 33

ARTIST
Dave Allsop

MEDIUM USED
Digital

CARD NAME

Onyxia (Stage 3)

Onyxia Raid 3 / 33

ARTIST
Mauro Cascioli

MEDIUM USED
Digital

CARD NAME

Frost Trap
Dark Portal 33 / 319

ARTIST
Dan Scott

MEDIUM USED
Digital

M&L

222

CARD NAME

Penelope's Rose
Dark Portal 266 / 319

ARTIST

Terese Nielsen

MEDIUM USED

Acrylic

CARD NAME
Manhunt
Dark Portal 291 / 319

ARTIST
Ralph Horsley

MEDIUM USED
Acrylic

CARD NAME
Boat to Booty Bay
Dark Portal 138 / 319

ARTIST
Peter Lee

MEDIUM USED
Digital

M&L

CARD NAME
Wanted: "Hogger"
Dark Portal 299 / 319

ARTIST
Sean O'Daniels

MEDIUM USED
Digital

CARD NAME

King Mukla
Dark Portal 244 / 319

ARTIST
Sunny

MEDIUM USED
Digital

CARD NAME

Fortune Telling
Dark Portal 143 / 319

ARTISTS
Glenn Rane & Ben Brode

MEDIUM USED
Digital

CARD NAME
Poison Water
Dark Portal 305 / 319

ARTISTS
Zoltan Boros & Gabor Szikszai

MEDIUM USED
Mixed (Acrylic + Digital)

CARD NAME
Shred Soul
Dark Portal 114 / 319

ARTIST
Cos Koniotis

MEDIUM USED
Digital

CARD NAME

The Lobotomizer
Dark Portal 278 / 319

ARTIST
Michael Sutfin

MEDIUM USED
Oil

CARD NAME

Lokholar the Ice Lord
Dark Portal 222 / 319

ARTIST
Dan Scott

MEDIUM USED
Digital

CARD NAME

Flames of the Incinerator
Molten Core Raid 20 / 53

ARTIST
Kev Walker

MEDIUM USED
Gouache

CARD NAME
Scimitar of the
Nexus Stalkers
Dark Portal 280 / 319

ARTIST
Patrick McEvoy

MEDIUM USED
Digital

CARD NAME
Zin'rokh, Destroyer of Worlds
Dark Portal 288 / 319

ARTIST
Richard Wright

MEDIUM USED
Digital

M&L

CARD NAME

Stitches

Dark Portal 246 / 319

ARTIST

Trevor Jacobs

MEDIUM USED

Digital

CARD NAME

Overseer Oilfist
Dark Portal 245 / 319

ARTIST
Scott Hampton

MEDIUM USED
Watercolor

CARD NAME

Plagueborn Meatwall
Dark Portal 228 / 319

ARTIST
Dave Allsop

MEDIUM USED
Oil

CARD NAME
Spellbreaker's Buckler
Outland 205 / 246

ARTIST
Richard Wright

MEDIUM USED
Digital

CARD NAME
Anger Management
Dark Portal 115 / 319

ARTIST
Jun Kang

MEDIUM USED
Digital

CARD NAME
Reaver of the Infinites
Outland 217 / 246

ARTIST
Greg Staples

MEDIUM USED
Digital

M&I

CARD NAME
Doomguard
Dark Portal 104 / 319

ARTIST
Carl Critchlow

MEDIUM USED
Acrylic

CARD NAME
Spectral Tiger
Outland Loot 3 / 3

ARTIST
Raven Mimura

MEDIUM USED
Digital

M&L

CARD NAME
Eye of Kilrogg
Dark Portal 105 / 319

ARTIST
Clint Langley

MEDIUM USED
Digital

CARD NAME
Jin'do's Bag of Whammies
Dark Portal 263 / 319

ARTIST
Jeff Easley

MEDIUM USED
Oil

CARD NAME

Obsidian Edged Blade
Molten Core 24 / 30

ARTIST
Luca Zontini

MEDIUM USED
Acrylic

CARD NAME

Legplates of Wrath
Molten Core 7 / 30

ARTIST
Lucas Graciano

MEDIUM USED
Oil

CARD NAME

Core Hound Tooth
Molten Core 20 / 30

ARTIST
Michael Sutfin

MEDIUM USED
Oil

CARD NAME
Garr (front)
Molten Core Raid 4 / 53

ARTIST
Ben Wootten

MEDIUM USED
Digital

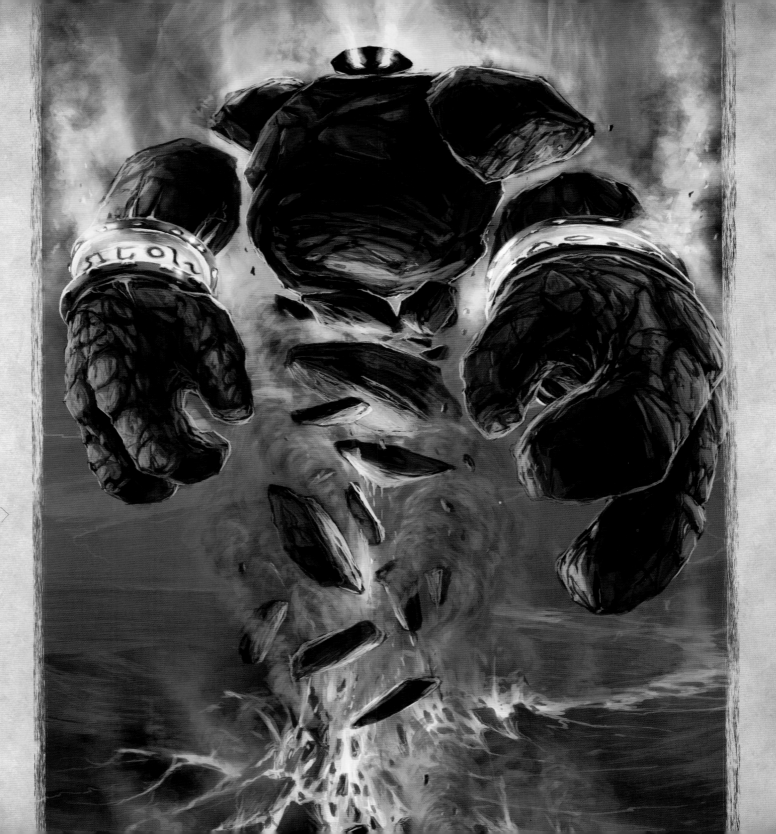

CARD NAME
Garr (back)
Molten Core Raid 4 / 53

ARTIST
Ben Wootten

MEDIUM USED
Digital

CARD NAME

Baron Geddon
Molten Core Raid 5 / 53

ARTIST

Brandon Kitkouski

MEDIUM USED

Digital

CARD NAME

Golemagg the Incinerator
Molten Core Raid 8 / 53

ARTIST

Glenn Rane

MEDIUM USED

Digital

M&I

247

CARD NAME
Baron Geddon (back)
Molten Core Raid 5 / 53

ARTIST
Brandon Kitkouski

MEDIUM USED
Digital

CARD NAME
Firelord
Molten Core Raid 34 / 53

ARTIST
Michael Komarck

MEDIUM USED
Digital

CARD NAME
Molten Giants
Molten Core Raid 40 / 53

ARTIST
John Avon

MEDIUM USED
Digital

CARD NAME
Hellreaver
Dark Portal 276 / 319

ARTIST
Patrick McEvoy

MEDIUM USED
Digital

CARD NAME
Firesworn
Molten Core Token 1 / 6

ARTIST
Ben Wootten

MEDIUM USED
Digital

CARD NAME

Golemagg the Incinerator
Molten Core Raid 8 / 53

ARTIST
Glenn Rane

MEDIUM USED
Digital

CARD NAME
Sulfuron Harbinger (back)
Molten Core Raid 7 / 53

ARTIST
Eric Browning

MEDIUM USED
Digital

CARD NAME

Sulfuron Harbinger (front)

Molten Core Raid 7 / 53

ARTIST

Eric Browning

MEDIUM USED

Digital

Gehennas (front)
Molten Core Raid 3 / 53

ARTIST
Alex Horley Orlandelli

MEDIUM USED
Acrylic

CARD NAME

Gehennas (back)
Molten Core Raid 3 / 53

ARTIST
Alex Horley Orlandelli

MEDIUM USED
Acrylic

CARD NAME

Inspire
Molten Core Raid 23 / 53

ARTIST
Phroilan Gardner

MEDIUM USED
Digital

CARD NAME
Lucifron (front)
Molten Core Raid 1 / 53

ARTIST
Aleksi Briclot

MEDIUM USED
Digital

CARD NAME
Lucifron (back)
Molten Core Raid 1 / 53

ARTIST
Aleksi Briclot

MEDIUM USED
Digital

Ancient Core Hound

Molten Core Raid 33 / 53

ARTIST
E.M. Gist

MEDIUM USED
Oil

CARD NAME
Magmadar
Molten Core Raid 2 / 53

ARTIST
Clint Langley

MEDIUM USED
Digital

CARD NAME
Flaming Assault
Molten Core Raid 45 / 53

ARTIST
Puddnhead

MEDIUM USED
Digital

CARD NAME
Wrath of Ragnaros
Molten Core Raid 53 / 53

ARTIST
Michael Komarck

MEDIUM USED
Digital

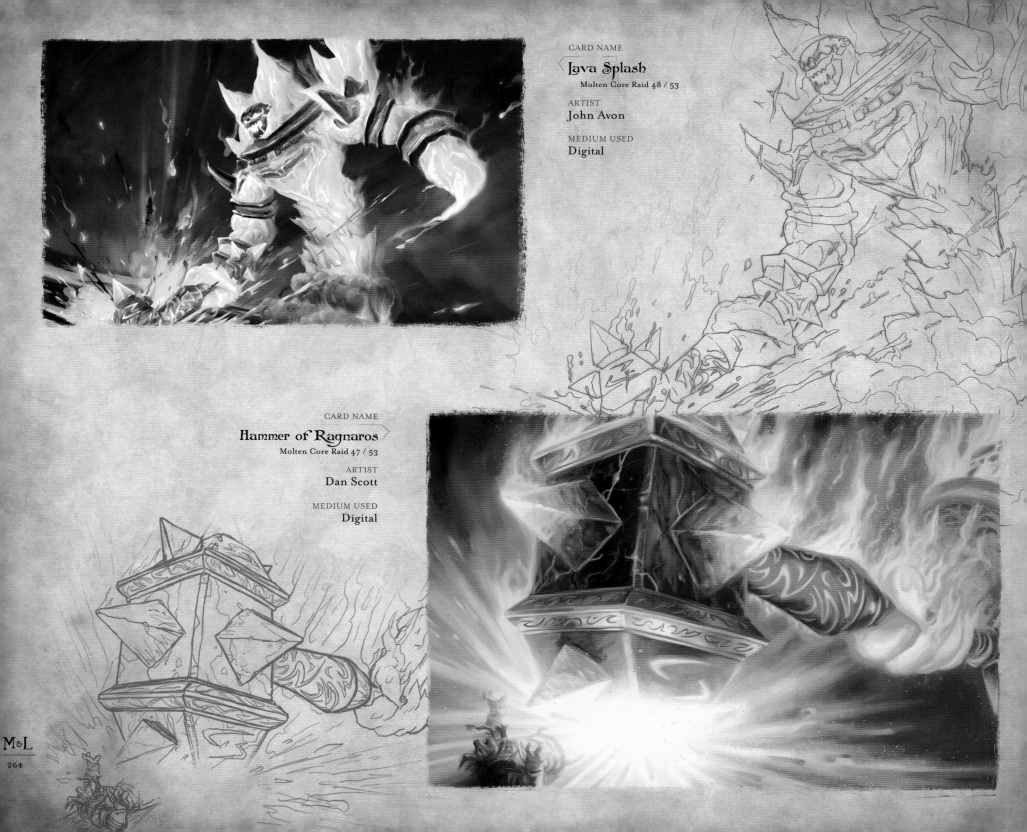

CARD NAME
Lava Splash
Molten Core Raid 48 / 53

ARTIST
John Avon

MEDIUM USED
Digital

CARD NAME
Hammer of Ragnaros
Molten Core Raid 47 / 53

ARTIST
Dan Scott

MEDIUM USED
Digital

M&L

CARD NAME
Magma Blast
Molten Core Raid 49 / 53

ARTIST
Jonboy Meyers

MEDIUM USED
Digital

CARD NAME
Fury of the Firelord
Molten Core Raid 46 / 53

ARTIST
Brandon Kitkouski

MEDIUM USED
Digital

CARD NAME
Ragnaros
Molten Core Raid 10 / 53

ARTIST
Greg Staples

MEDIUM USED
Digital

CARD NAME
Ragnaros
Molten Coe Raid 10 / 53

ARTIST
Peter Lee

MEDIUM USED
Digital

M&L

CARD NAME

Chen Stormstout
Outland 192 / 246

ARTIST
Samwise

MEDIUM USED
Digital

CARD NAME

"He Who Has No Life"
Outland 121 / 246

ARTIST
Daren Bader

MEDIUM USED
Digital

CARD NAME

Angrida
Outland 82 / 246

ARTIST
Glenn Rane

MEDIUM USED
Digital

CARD NAME

Sword of a Thousand Truths
Outland 223 / 246

ARTIST
Peter Lee

MEDIUM USED
Digital

CARD NAME

Corki's Ransom
Outland 227 / 246

ARTIST
James Zhang

MEDIUM USED
Digital

CARD NAME

Aldori Legacy Defender
Outland 194 / 246

ARTIST
Peter Lee

MEDIUM USED
Digital

CARD NAME

Force of Nature
Outland 22 / 246

ARTIST
Trevor Jacobs

MEDIUM USED
Digital

CARD NAME
Nightfire
Outland 32 / 246

ARTIST
Randy Gallegos

MEDIUM USED
Oil

CARD NAME
The Fare of Jar'korwi
Outland 233 / 246

ARTIST
Alex Horley Orlandelli

MEDIUM USED
Acrylic

Terrifying Presence
Magtheridon's Lair Raid 27 / 43

ARTIST
Greg Staples

MEDIUM USED
Digital

CARD NAME

Magtheridon's Rage
Magtheridon's Lair Raid 15 / 43

ARTISTS
Zoltan Boros &
Gabor Szikszai

MEDIUM USED
Mixed (Acrylic + Oil)

M&L

CARD NAME
Manticron Cube
Magtheridon's Lair Raid 42 / 43

ARTIST
Peter Lee

MEDIUM USED
Digital

CARD NAME
Magtheridon
Magtheridon's Lair Raid 43 / 43

ARTIST
Glenn Rane

MEDIUM USED
Digital

CARD NAME
Hellfire Channeler
Magtheridon's Lair Raid 35 / 43

ARTISTS
Zoltan Boros &
Gabor Szikszai

MEDIUM USED
Mixed (Acrylic + Digital)

M&I

Acknowledgments

As the World of Warcraft® Trading Card Game moved through development, we realized that beyond creating a top-notch game, we also were amassing a world-class collection of fantasy art—a collection that we thought would be appreciated by *World of Warcraft* gamers and art aficionados alike.

It goes without saying that this project would never have happened without the visionary talents of Blizzard Entertainment®, who created such a rich and compelling world. Thank you to Samwise Didier, Glenn Rane, Ben Brode, Shawn Carnes, Sean Wang, Brian Hsieh, Cory Jones, and Gloria Soto, whose contributions helped make this book possible.

Behind every great book is a great book publisher. From Chronicle Books, our great thanks go out to Catherine Huchting and Kevin Toyama for their enthusiasm and support from day one; the tireless work of Pamela Geismar, Jane Chinn, and Beth Weber; the careful eyes of Laurel Leigh and Corey Cohen; and to our outstanding designers, Robert J. Williams and Melissa Tioleco-Cheng of RISE-AND-SHINE STUDIO.

At Upper Deck, a special thanks to David Lomeli, Brian Bateman, and Marco Sipriaso for their creative vision; Brandon Male, Cate Muscat, Rob Vaux, and Stan! for their content expertise; Brian Bayne for keeping us on schedule; Jeremy Cranford for carrying the vision of *World of Warcraft* and communicating that vision to the artists; Dan Bojanowski and the rest of the *World of Warcraft* brand team for keeping everyone focused on the spirit of the game; Tim Muret for believing in this project from the start; and Susan Theodore for managing this book from concept to reality and every step in between.

Of course, great thanks and deep respect go out to all the artists who worked on the World of Warcraft TCG. This book is a testament to the time, energy, and love you brought to our game.

Last, but certainly not least, thank you to all of the *World of Warcraft* gaming enthusiasts. None of this would have been possible without your devotion and support.

BLIZZARD ENTERTAINMENT CREDITS:

ART DIRECTOR: Glenn Rane

PRODUCER: Ben Brode

ASSOCIATE PRODUCER: Sean Wang

CREATIVE DEVELOPMENT MANAGER: Shawn Carnes

DIRECTOR, GLOBAL BUSINESS DEVELOPMENT AND LICENSING: Cory Jones

LICENSING MANAGERS: Gina Williams, Brian Hsieh

SPECIAL THANKS TO: Chris Metzen, Gloria Soto, Stuart Massie, Joanna Cleland-Jolly, Justin Parker, Peter C. Lee, Micky Neilsen, Evelyn Fredericksen, and Elizabeth Cho

Artist Index

Card Title Index